The Accusers

The Accusers

LYNN L. CLARK

The Plaid Raccoon Press
2016

The Accusers is a work of fiction. All names, characters, institutions, places and events portrayed in this novel are either the product of the author's imagination or are used fictitiously. Any resemblance to actual persons, living or dead, events or locales is entirely coincidental.

For my niece, Heather Jones,
who continues to amaze me with
her intelligence, compassion,
and sense of humour. This
novel is for you, Heather.
I hope you like it.

1

Berwick Street was a quiet cul-de-sac. Most of its residents were middle-aged couples or seniors who had owned their houses for years. Lovely old oak trees provided shade in summer, and there was a playground at the end of the street. This winter, it boasted an outdoor skating rink, thanks to Mr. Scott, a recent retiree who was finding it difficult to make the transition from workplace to home.

But something strange was happening on this sleepy little street in this average little town. Something that threatened to leave no survivors.

2

Rebecca   Anderson,   affectionately known as Becca by family and friends, was a pleasant-faced woman, short and a bit plump, with curly grey hair. She was usually quick to smile, but today her expression was one of sadness. She turned on a reading lamp as she sat in her living room. It was February: the shortest, yet longest month of the year. The last rays of the winter sun had already died, and it was only 5 PM. According to the local news channel, there was heavy snow in the forecast.

Becca didn't understand the depression she'd been experiencing lately. She'd lived in this house on Berwick Street for forty years and had raised three children here with the help of her beloved husband Jack, dead of cancer for five years now. She'd always tried to see the best in people and circumstances. After all, the house was paid for and she had a pension, supplemented by the money she earned from her baking, which was sold at a local shop and was renowned throughout the township. Her oldest daughter Leah, who taught at a university on the west coast, had a delightful and precocious little girl named Charlotte. Jim, the middle child, was an attorney in Ottawa. Elizabeth, the youngest, lived with her partner in a nearby village and worked as a freelance graphic artist. Becca's children had purchased a laptop for her two years ago, and she was able to use Facebook and Skype to keep in touch with them.

Becca put aside the Kobo the children had bought her this Christmas because they knew she loved to read. She was starting to get the hang of the device, although she much preferred the feel of a book in her hands.

She headed for the kitchen to begin preparing her supper. Her constant shadow, Mooch the cat, was nowhere to be seen.

He must be sleeping somewhere.

Becca pulled the cutting board from the cupboard and started assembling ingredients for a salad. She searched for the knife she always used to cut vegetables, but it wasn't in the butcher's block or the dishwasher.

Strange. I'm only sixty-five. I hope I'm not starting to get forgetful and misplacing things.

She selected another knife and began to slice the lettuce and tomatoes, trying to pinpoint when exactly this depressed feeling had started. Was it the usual letdown when the kids left after being home for the holidays? No, it had started earlier than that. She remembered the moment now. Charlotte had been sitting on her lap, telling her about her best friends at kindergarten when she'd suddenly asked, "Where'd the spirit go, Grandma?"

"What do you mean, Charlotte?"

"The Christmas spirit. There aren't any lights out on your street, 'cept yours. And where's the sleigh with Santa and all his presents? I saw it last year. It blew up like a big balloon at night."

And then Becca had realized the child was right. There were no twinkling lights to see, no inflatables, no wreaths in a neighbourhood that had always prided itself on its elaborate Christmas displays.

The depression had started then, accompanied by an urgent sense of foreboding that all was not right on quiet Berwick Street.

Her thoughts were interrupted by a loud

thump outside on the porch. Becca wiped her hands on a dish towel and hurried to the door.

When she opened it, she found a note pinned there with her missing knife. Her hands shaking, she removed the knife and read the note.

You have been marked.

She spotted Mooch under the living room couch. The cat was hissing violently in fright, but there was no one to be seen on the street nor were there footprints in the crusted snow.

3

Mabel Wright, a tall, thin, white-haired woman in her mid-eighties, opened her front door and walked gingerly outside onto the verandah. The sky was moisture-laden with impending snow. She could feel it in her bones. She stamped her cane on the floor of the verandah as if that act alone could stop the storm dead in its tracks.

Because of her limited mobility, the local community centre sent volunteers to visit Mabel twice a week, and she had Meals on Wheels at least three times weekly. The rest she prepared herself.

The young, pretty volunteers who came to her house were at times intimidated by her and at other times amazed at her powers of recall.

"Father always said I had a mind like a steel trap, except for things that don't bear remembering," she'd tell them and then proceed to discuss poetry or art or whatever subject struck her fancy. She'd been a school teacher for thirty years before retiring and had loved working with children. She'd been very strict, putting up with no nonsense in the classroom, but her students always respected her. Many of them remembered her with affection and still sent her Christmas cards each year.

Mabel's own children and her husband had died many years ago, leaving her with an unspoken sorrow. But she had moved on with her life as best she could and believed she still had a few good years ahead of her in spite of her osteoporosis.

Damn snow never ends. I hate it. I hate being afraid of falling. I've never been afraid of anything in my life.

But—truth be told—Mabel knew she was just whistling in the dark.

Something had her spooked. She was very afraid, and it had nothing to do with a possible fall on the ice.

4

Fourteen-year-old Nick Harris, a freckle-faced boy with brown hair and piercing blue eyes, was playing a video game online and getting zapped right, left, and centre. Normally he could anticipate his opponent's every move, but he wasn't concentrating on the screen.

Stupid game, stupid, stupid cast.

Nick had broken his left leg during a pick-up hockey game on the rink that Mr. Scott had laboured to build. Now he would miss the whole hockey season. Worse still, his mom was hovering over him all the time, asking him how he felt and whether he was comfortable. And his friends all laughed at him as he slipped and slid on his crutches and struggled to board the school bus.

This sucks.

But a voice in his head told him that there were things much worse than having a broken leg. Much worse indeed.

5

Cassie Patterson, a woman in her late twenties, had moved back to her hometown from the city to look after her ailing father. When he died and she inherited the house on Berwick Street, she'd decided to stay on rather than sell her childhood home. She was a potter by trade, selling her wares at various craft shows and fairs, but she also worked full time at a local grocery store.

Cassie had been only five years old when her mother died. To compensate for her loneliness while her father was away at work, she'd spent hours reading at the local library when she was not in school. Along the way, she'd developed a special interest in religion and the supernatural, devouring every book she could find on spiritualism and the occult.

Before her mother's death, she and Cassie had been inseparable. She still had memories of her mother sitting at the table with a special board spread in front of her.

"What is it, Mommy? Is it magic?" she'd asked.

"Your daddy thinks it's silly, so it will be our secret, okay? It's a spirit board that helps me feel very close to people who aren't with me now. Does that make sense, sweetheart?"

Cassie had nodded knowingly, feeling like a big girl for sharing the secret of the board with her mother, although in truth she wondered why Mommy didn't just call these people on the telephone.

When she was ten years old and had been rooting in the attic for skates, Cassie found her mother's old Ouija board. She patiently learned how to use it. To this day, she believed in the power of the board, rejecting the scientific explanation that the ideomotor reflex—unconscious movement by the board's users—was responsible for the messages the wooden pointer, the planchette, spelled out. And she dismissed as superstition the belief that it was dangerous to use the Ouija board when alone.

Her secret hope was to connect with

her mother's spirit, although that had not yet happened. She'd managed, however, to contact three others in the spirit world. There was Dietrich, who'd died centuries ago, and Edward, who'd met an untimely death in a car accident. More recently, Jana, who'd been killed in an airplane crash, had reached out to her.

This evening Cassie had been drawn to the board. She'd removed it from its usual resting place on top of her bookcase, setting it up on her dining room table.

For the last hour there had been no movement, but suddenly the planchette on which she rested her fingers began to glide across the board and slowly spell out its message.

This time it was Dietrich who was communicating with her. She could feel his presence.

Tonight his message read:

Death is coming.

6

Sunday Evening, nearing midnight

The self-appointed Guardians of Truth sat in a circle in the damp, abandoned building they had chosen for their meeting place. They had selected James Sampson, a short man with thin lips and severe features, as their leader. At forty-two, he was much younger than some of the others in the group, but they believed he deserved the leadership. It had been Sampson's grandfather and father who'd lured all of the residents of Berwick Street to that location. It had been painstaking work—planning, falsifying documents of title, intervening in events, making sure that no one escaped his or her fate. And the deaths the Guardians had engineered thus far had not aroused any suspicions on the part of the authorities.

Except for the newer members who were still cultivating their skills, each of the group had special abilities. Donald Grierson, who was seventy years old and the longest-serving member of the group, had the power of telekinesis, allowing him to move objects with his mind. He had been a friend of Sampson's father.

Angus Motts, another long-time member of the group, thought of himself as the silver-tongued devil. He had the ability to influence thoughts and had caused several youths on Berwick Street to commit reckless acts resulting in death.

Scott Napier, a particularly sadistic man who had abandoned any pretense to conscience, had the power of pyrokinesis and had succeeded in causing the deaths of many older Berwick Street residents by setting fires that were ruled accidental.

Roland Fian, the second-in-command, had the power of remote viewing—the ability to see things in his mind from a distance. He had always been a thoughtful man, taking no pleasure in imposing a death sentence on Berwick Street residents, but trying to maintain a stoic belief that his actions were the inevitable result of a four-century-old tragedy.

Their leader James Sampson had the

greatest ability of them all. He was schooled in the dark arts and was able to harness the powers of the Ancient Ones—Satan and his league of demons—to carry out his evil tasks. He was relentless in his pursuit of their cause, never displaying weakness to his followers or engaging in feelings of remorse.

Sampson signalled for silence and told the gathering, "A storm at sea precipitated this chaos, and another storm will end it. A perfect symmetry."

"Do we expect any resistance?" asked Roland Fian, a man more than twenty years older than Sampson but his closest, and perhaps only, friend.

"There are four among them that have precognitive abilities, and we must not overlook their potential influence. But the women who've already anticipated our coming are old, and we've scared one of them badly with our message on her door. And the young boy can't do much now, seeing as he's lugging around a plaster cast after his *unfortunate* fall on the skating rink."

Sampson paused for effect and the younger members of the group laughed nervously. In fact they were terrified of Sampson and his ruthlessness.

"There is a younger woman, however, who may prove a bit harder to defeat. I suspect she's always known subconsciously that her mother's death wasn't a natural one. She has studied for years and possesses an abundance of as-yet-untapped abilities. And her cursed Ouija board has already spelled out a warning to her.

"But in the end we will prevail."

7

Monday Morning, 10 AM

The storm began quietly enough over-night with only a few snowflakes falling languidly to the pavement. By 4 AM, however, there were more than fifty centimetres of snow on the ground. The wind played havoc with it, whipping it into huge drifts and creating whiteouts for drivers. Already there had been several accidents.

The wind also blew down power lines, causing temporary blackouts in most parts of the town.

The hydro workers repairing the lines noticed an eerie silence when they arrived at Berwick Street that morning. No one was digging out a car, no children were playing outside even though the school buses had been cancelled, and there was no one looking out windows to see what was happening outside. The workers were inexplicably relieved to move on to their next job.

Becca and her cat Mooch sat bundled together under several quilts.

Mabel, who had an old cast-iron wood stove, was stoking the fire.

Cassie was moving aimlessly from room to room, still unnerved by the message from Dietrich.

Nick was sleeping in because of the school bus cancellations, but his mind was restless as he battled unseen invaders in his dreams.

8

Monday Morning, 11 AM

Becca was talking to her daughter Leah, who'd called to see how her mother was doing when she saw the storm warnings on the national weather site. "Mom, you really should come out here for a while. We've got hardly any snow. Charlotte would love to have you here. She's still talking about her Christmas visit."

"Oh well, I don't think I'd fit in among the west coasters"—she always thought of British Columbia as la-la land, but had never shared this thought with her daughter. "Besides, I've got lots of groceries in the house and the power's on now. If it goes off again, I can always go over to Mabel's house. She has that old wood stove."

Leah sighed. "Mom, what is it you're not

telling me? Your voice is off."

"Probably just a winter cold. Nothing to worry about."

"You know that's not what I mean. Your voice has got that edge to it. Like you're worried about something. I heard it enough growing up in that house. What's got you spooked?"

"Well, it seems as if my old lightning rod's working again"—that was the term they'd used for Becca's uncanny ability to predict events. In fact, she'd known before the police called her when Leah, still a teenager, had slid off the road after her car hit a patch of black ice. And she'd sensed that death was imminent for her seemingly healthy grandmother, who died suddenly of an aneurysm. The list went on and on.

Leah had witnessed her mother's ability too many times to take it lightly. "What is it you're seeing, Mom?"

"It's so vague this time, Leah. That's what frustrates me the most. It's just a sense of foreboding. As if everything's off somehow. Even Charlotte sensed it at Christmas." Becca went on to tell Leah of Charlotte's insistence that the Christmas spirit was missing in action. She omitted any mention of the stolen knife and the note on her door. She didn't want to alarm her daughter.

There was silence on the other end of the line. "Leah, are you still there?"

Leah finally spoke. "That accounts for it, then. Since we've returned, Charlotte's been asking me over and over if Grandma's okay because some mean person killed the spirit."

9

Cassie checked the lock twice before heading for her car to go to work for her afternoon shift. Not that there was much to steal in her house, but it was more a question of what she wanted to keep *out*. She wasn't certain from which direction the danger would come, but intended to remain hyper-vigilant.

She cleared the snow from the car's windows, running the motor and waiting for the vehicle to warm up. The snowplow had recently deposited clumps of frozen snow at the end of her driveway. She grabbed the shovel from the side of her house and began clearing them away. They were heavy and it was hard work to remove them.

As if steered by an unseen presence,

Cassie's automobile slipped into reverse and began to back down the long driveway, gaining momentum as it went. She sensed—rather than saw—the car coming toward her, instinctively scrambling out of its path before it jumped the curb and stalled in a nearby snowbank.

******

The tow truck came after an hour's wait. The driver apologized for the delay, explaining that the snowstorm was resulting in additional calls for cars that were stuck or had spun out on the roads. He lowered the hook from his truck with an electric winch and fastened it to the front of Cassie's vehicle.

"If you'd like to hitch a ride with me into town, I can drop you off wherever you were headed."

"Thanks. I'd appreciate that. And could you please tow my car to the GM dealership? I've already called and they said they'd have a mechanic check it out."

On the way into town, Cassie explained to the tow truck driver how her car had shifted suddenly into reverse gear.

The driver shook his head. "That's a new one on me."

10

Mabel dozed in her rocking chair by the wood stove, her hand still resting on the head of her dog Tex, a chocolate Lab. She loved this dog with all her heart, had raised it from a puppy, and had even left explicit instructions for his care once she was gone. In turn the dog was completely devoted to his mistress.

Tex raised his head, sniffed, and emitted a low growl from the back of his throat.

The man who'd been watching the two of them from outside Mabel's kitchen window cursed, ducked quickly, and then disappeared without a trace.

11

Nick was bored. He'd been playing video games all day now, but his heart wasn't really in it.

He'd stopped for a while and was now sending messages to his friends through Facebook.

Suddenly a new message appeared in the middle of the screen:

> *Old Mrs. Wright's in trouble,*
> *get help, get help, HELP....*

His gut instinct told him this was true.

His mom was at work so he grabbed his cellphone from the desk and punched in 911.

By the time the ambulance arrived,

Mabel and her dog were unconscious from carbon monoxide fumes. All the paramedics could do now was to administer oxygen and hope for the best.

12

Monday Afternoon, 4:25 PM

Becca heard the shrill whine of the ambulance siren and rushed quickly to her kitchen window to look outside. The ambulance had stopped at Mabel Wright's house. A heart attack, maybe?

She watched as a paramedic wheeled the old woman from her house, and another attendant carried Mabel's dog outside. Now the ambulance crew was administering oxygen to both of them.

From her vantage point she couldn't tell whether either of them was responding.

******

Seeing the ambulance, Al Scott hurried outside to talk to the paramedics. Mabel and her dog had rallied with the oxygen, but the ambulance attendants told him they would still be taking Mabel to the hospital to make sure she'd be okay.

The ambulance driver explained that they thought the wood stove was the source of the carbon monoxide poisoning. "The pipes are probably clogged with soot."

Al looked troubled but said nothing. *Can't see how there could have been a build-up of soot. I cleaned the pipes out for her just last week.*

"Is there anyone who can take the dog to a vet to have him examined?" the driver asked as the ambulance was about to leave.

"I'll look after him," Al replied. "Just take good care of Mabel. C'mon, Tex. Let's get you checked out. Then you can stay with the missus and me for a while." He gently placed the dog in his pick-up truck, covered him with blankets that he kept in the vehicle for emergencies, and headed for the local vet.

13

It was a busy shift for Cassie as a steady stream of customers came into the grocery store to pick up extra water, batteries, and canned goods to get them through the storm. The snow had abated, but there was more in the forecast.

When her break came, she grabbed her cellphone and called the dealership to ask about her car.

"Couldn't find a thing wrong with it, and there's no manufacturer's recall for a problem like that. You can pick it up any time."

"You'll be closed by the time my shift ends. I'll pick it up in the morning. I'll be there around 9:30."

As she ended the call, Cassie realized she

wasn't surprised to hear there was no defect in her car. She'd already surmised that the shifting of gears in the vehicle had nothing to do with auto mechanics.

Someone had tried to kill her.

14

Monday Evening, 7-8 PM

The hospital was keeping Mabel at least overnight for observation. As Al Scott entered the hospital room, he took Mabel's hand and quickly reassured her that Tex had been checked out and was sleeping soundly. His wife was keeping an eye out, just to make sure the dog was okay.

The lighting in the room cast a harsh glow on the bed and made Mabel look even older than her eighty-four years. Her skin was chalky white and she coughed intermittently.

"Thank you so much, Al. You know how much Tex means to me. There's only the two of us."

"Mabel, I've talked it over with Doreen, and we want you to stay with us for a few days once you get out of the hospital. You've had a terrible shock, and if it weren't for the Harris kid, well—"

"I don't understand, Al."

"The Harris boy called 911. Don't ask me how he knew to call. His mother's still trying to puzzle it out, but the boy's pretty shaken up and doesn't want to talk about it."

******

The second visitor that evening was Becca, who brought a large bouquet of flowers with her. She got a vase from the nurses' station and fussed with the flowers, as if trying to avoid talking for the moment.

"You *know*, don't you, Becca?"

"Know what, Mabel?"

"You and I always had a sixth sense about us. And we both know something really, really bad is happening. Here, look at this. I got Al Scott to bring it in for me. I know for sure that what happened to me wasn't an accident, and my gut tells me that it's got to do with this." Mabel reached for a wooden box on her bedside table and withdrew a yellowed sheet of paper from it. It looked like a page from an old history book. "I found this in my husband's belongings after he died. While he was alive, he never once mentioned it to me, but he obviously believed it was important enough to keep all those years." She handed the paper to Becca.

The other woman started reading the faded text and then looked up at Mabel. "I don't understand. This is about a town in Scotland. It was horrible what they did, but how does it possibly relate to us?"

"Look at the *name* of the town, Becca. And the surnames of the townspeople."

Becca glanced again at the paper. "But, I mean, after all these years. The victims are all long dead."

"But their descendants aren't."

"So you think it's—revenge? Does it make any sense for something that happened four centuries ago?"

But even as she protested, Becca knew in her heart that Mabel was right.

God help us. God help us all.

15

Cassie knocked timidly on the door of the Anderson house. Becca opened it cautiously on the chain lock and, relieved to see who it was, slid back the chain and invited Cassie in.

"I hope I'm not visiting too late, Mrs. Anderson, but I just got dropped off from work and I saw your lights on. Al Scott came into the grocery store for a few things just as I was about to finish my shift and told me what happened to Mabel Wright. I was so sad to hear about it. Mrs. Wright was wonderful to my dad and me when he was ill. She'd often sit by his bedside when he was too weak to get up and talk softly to him about what she called 'gentler' times."

"Mabel would be touched by your

concern, Cassie." Becca smiled graciously at the young woman. "Come in and have a seat. I've got some decaffeinated tea brewing. Would you like a cup?"

"That would be lovely as long as it's no bother," Cassie said as she removed her boots and left them on the tray by the door. "I've been meaning to visit more often, but with work and all," she shrugged apologetically. "I did see Elizabeth when she was home for Christmas"—the two of them had been classmates. "She said you were keeping well. Very busy with the sale of your baked goods."

Cassie sat on the couch while Becca, declining her offer of help with a smile and reassurance that it was no bother, went to the kitchen to pour the tea.

Mooch jumped up on Cassie's lap and began purring noisily as she patted him.

Becca brought a tray with the tea and some cookies and set it on the coffee table. She laughed as she poured a cup for the young woman. "I see you're being honoured by His Majesty's presence. He must sense that you like animals. He's usually pretty standoffish with company."

Cassie reached for the cup of tea Becca offered her. "I've loved animals since I was little. Mom always said a person who loves animals has a kind heart and a clear conscience. I'm not sure about that saying, but she did teach me to respect all living things."

"That's a very important lesson to teach a child," Becca said.

Cassie smiled and nodded. "By the way, Mr. Scott told me you went to see Mrs. Wright this evening. How was she?"

A look of worry momentarily crossed Becca's face. "She was … agitated, of course, after the close call. Typically, she was more concerned about her dog Tex than herself. She dotes on that animal."

"I'm not sure how to say this, Mrs. Anderson, so I'll just come out with it. Elizabeth used to tell me how you were able to … predict events. My mom had that ability too, and I think, well, maybe I've inherited it. What I want to know is whether everything seems … all right to you."

Becca heaved a huge sigh and said, "No, Cassie, things are definitely *not* all right." And then she began to unburden herself of her fears, telling the young woman about the document Mabel Wright had shared with her.

16

Monday Evening, 10 PM

Nick was very, very scared. It was happening again. It was like when he was a little kid and Joey went missing and Nick knew that he had been exploring Mr. Acton's old barn and had fallen through some rotten boards. Nick had been too afraid at the time to say anything, but sure enough they'd found Joey in the barn, and he'd been okay, just frightened. And now it was happening all over again.

His mom peeked into his room and saw that he was still awake. "Do you want to talk about what happened, Nick?"

"Is Mrs. Wright okay, Mom? I know she's really, really old."

His mother affectionately brushed the hair out of his eyes, a gesture that Nick partly hated because it made him feel like a baby and partly liked because he knew how much his mom loved him. "She's fine, Nick. Thanks to you. But how did you know to call 911?"

Nick shrugged. Then he decided to tell his mother the truth. "I got a warning on Facebook that she was in trouble. See, here it is."

But when he called up his Facebook page, the urgent message telling him to call 911 had disappeared.

17

James Sampson scowled at his followers. He had called an emergency meeting, and the Guardians of Truth were once again assembled in the abandoned structure they'd claimed as their meeting place.

"This is not going according to plan. Somehow that boy managed to alert the authorities to the old woman's condition, and that young woman dodged the car.

"This is ridiculous," Sampson continued. "All this planning by our forefathers and we're taking this long to complete the final step. And there are only four of them. Three women and a boy, for pity's sake!"

He eyed Geoffrey Thompson, who had been responsible for engineering the deaths of both women, with a look of scorn.

Thompson clenched his fists and stared angrily at his lap, but said nothing. He knew better than to offer excuses. Many of them had already tasted Sampson's wrath. The two empty seats at the table could attest to its power.

"Okay," Sampson continued. "We've obviously underestimated their strength. Make sure it doesn't happen again." He discussed their next moves and then dismissed the group.

Roland Fian waited until the others left so he could speak to Sampson.

"What is it, Roland?" Sampson asked.

"I think you're going to have to cut them some slack, James. I know Thompson screwed up, but he's young and he's the newest member. The young ones don't understand. They don't have our level of commitment to the cause. To be honest, I'm not even sure why they joined us in the first place—probably because their fathers were too old or infirm to continue as Guardians and bullied them until they thought they had no other choice."

"So you think I was too hard on that incompetent Thompson?"

"I think you just need to tread more lightly, James. That's all I'm saying."

18

Tuesday Morning, 10:30 AM

After their long talk into the early morning hours, Becca and Cassie agreed that the two of them would have the best chance of mounting a resistance to any future attacks by sticking together.

Cassie picked up her car from the dealership and stopped by the grocery store to ask for a few days off. She then drove cautiously home and parked the car in her driveway. Afterward she packed and arrived at the Anderson house with her suitcase, laptop, and Ouija board to accept Becca's invitation to stay in one of her spare bedrooms.

As Becca showed Cassie to her room, she eyed the Ouija board. "Lord, I haven't seen one of those since I was a teenager. My friends and I used to play with one, and we'd all be giggling and blaming each other for moving the pointer."

Cassie was accustomed to this response to the spirit board. She could see that she would have some work to do convincing the older woman how important a tool it would be to them. She decided it was best to change the subject. "The young Harris boy, I think his name is Nick, obviously has precognitive abilities because he's the one who called 911 to save Mrs. Wright. Do you think we might be able to use his abilities to help us?"

Becca frowned. "He lives alone with his mother, and Edna's a very nervous person, one of those constant worriers. And the boy's had an accident recently. His leg's in a cast. I've seen him struggling to get on the school bus.

"But I can always do some baking and take it over as a 'thank you' on behalf of Mabel. I'm sure she'd be very happy if I did. She has so much trouble getting around in winter with her cane. I'll see if I can get a moment alone with Nick. I don't want to frighten him. I'll just try to find out how much he knows."

19

Tuesday Afternoon, 3 PM

Armed with peanut butter brownies and chocolate fudge, Becca headed to the Harris house.

Edna Harris was a widow. Her husband had been a truck driver and had died when his truck flipped over a guard rail and tumbled down a steep embankment. It was assumed that he'd fallen asleep at the wheel, although the Guardians of Truth would tell you otherwise. He had been in his late thirties. Now Edna was left to raise her son Nick on her own. Once a carefree teenager who used to be among Leah Anderson's circle of friends, Edna Harris had closed in on herself after her husband's death. She doted on her son Nick, but tended to be over-protective of him. Becca knew that she would have to tread very carefully.

"Mrs. Anderson, what a wonderful surprise. I haven't seen you in ages. Come in, come in," Edna greeted her and ushered her into the house, taking her coat and inviting her into the living room. It saddened Becca to see how shabby the furniture looked. Clearly Edna was struggling on her single income. Word was there'd only been enough insurance money to pay for her husband's burial expenses.

"Thanks, Edna. I hope I'm not intruding. I brought over some goodies for Nick. That was quick thinking on his part to call 911."

Edna's face clouded over. "How is Mrs. Wright doing? Is she still in the hospital? I hope there won't be any long-term effects."

"I heard from Al Scott that she'll be allowed to come home tomorrow. She'll stay with the Scotts until she gets back on her feet. I'm going to visit her tonight in the hospital so I'll pass on your best wishes.

"Would it be okay if I went to see Nick? I expect if he's like any other kid who has snow days from school he's in his room playing video games."

Edna laughed. "Right you are. I'll show you to his bedroom." She knocked on her son's closed door and then opened it. "Nick, we have a visitor. Mrs. Anderson is here to see you." Nick had his leg propped on a chair and looked to be engrossed in a video game. He switched it off as his mom and Mrs. Anderson entered his room.

"Hi, Nick. Neat cast you have. Can I sign it or do they do that any more?"

Nick thought it would be pretty dorky having his cast signed by an old lady but, always polite, he said, "Sure, Mrs. Anderson."

Becca sat on the edge of the bed—there didn't seem to be any other clear space in the room—and began to sign the cast with the Sharpie the boy handed her.

Edna looked embarrassed. She moved a stack of DVDs from a chair and beckoned her visitor to it. "Would you like a cup of tea, Mrs. Anderson?"

"I'd love one."

"I'll just run and make it then. You and Nick can catch up on the news. I'm sure he's anxious to hear about Mrs. Wright."

As soon as Edna was out of earshot, Becca turned to the boy. "That was a very brave thing you did, Nick. You saved Mrs. Wright's life and her dog's too. Do you feel up to telling me how you knew to call an ambulance?"

Nick swallowed hard and said, "I don't think you'll believe me, Mrs. Anderson. My mom thinks I'm making up a story."

"I think I *would* believe you, Nick. Why don't you tell me what happened?"

"I was on Facebook—sorry, do you know what that is, Mrs. Anderson?"

Becca smiled. "As a matter of fact, I do, Nick. I use it to talk to my children—they're grown up now and have all moved away—and to my grand-daughter Charlotte."

Nick looked embarrassed. "Well, I was talking to my friends and I got a message saying Mrs. Wright was in trouble. But now the message is gone."

"Has anything like this happened to you before, Nick? I mean that you knew ahead of time when something was wrong."

Nick hung his head and seemed reluctant to speak. Finally he said, "Well, a long time ago when I was just a kid, my friend Joey went missing, and I knew where he was. It was where they found him."

"Did you get a message that time?"

"It was more like a voice in my head telling me where to find Joey."

"You shouldn't be afraid of this, Nick. I have the same thing happen to me from time to time."

"Please don't say anything about this to my mom, Mrs. Anderson. She'll just worry."

"I won't talk to her about it, Nick. But

could you do me a favour?"

Nick nodded solemnly.

"I need your help and I know I can count on you. If you get any other ... warnings, could you please let me know right away?" She handed the boy a slip of paper with her phone number on it. "Any time, day or night. It's very important to me."

Nick reached for the paper and slipped it under his pillow just as his mother entered the room to announce that the tea was ready.

20

Tuesday Afternoon, 4:30 PM

Cassie had gone out for groceries, and Becca sat in her living room, trying unsuccessfully to concentrate on the book she was reading on her Kobo. She gave up, finally, and turned it off.

Did I do the right thing by involving a fourteen-year-old boy in all of this?

And what is the right thing, anyway?

All my life, I've tried to live by certain standards. I've tried to do the right thing by my husband and my children and friends, never really thinking about what that meant.

And now my whole world has been turned upside down.

I've promised Cassie that I'll help her. I don't want to let her down.

But what, realistically, can I do?

21

Cassie stamped the snow off her feet on the porch and suddenly felt awkward about the whole situation. Mrs. Anderson had given her a key, but she felt reluctant to use it. Her preference would have been to invite Mrs. Anderson to stay at her house, but the older woman had been reluctant to displace her cat Mooch. And, in truth, maybe she was better off here, surrounded by the wonderful smells of baking and the sense of security she'd always associated with this house. She hadn't been a close friend of Elizabeth, but she'd attended enough birthday parties here to remember that feeling of being safe as soon as she entered the Anderson house.

In the end, she didn't have to use the key. Becca opened the door and helped her in with the groceries, looking genuinely glad to see her.

After they'd put the groceries away, they sat in the living room, and Becca recounted the details of her visit with the Harrises.

Cassie nodded approvingly. "You handled it very well, Mrs. Anderson. Just like a pro. You didn't upset Edna, and at the same time you let Nick know that there was someone to turn to, someone who believed in him. I expect he'll sleep much better tonight knowing that."

"Thanks, Cassie. I was having a lot of doubts about whether I'd done the right thing. By the way, they're going to discharge Mabel Wright from the hospital tomorrow, but I'd like to go see her tonight just to have a chance to talk to her before she goes to the Scotts. They're good people, but strictly meat and potato folks. They'd probably think we're all crazy if we told them what we suspected was happening. Anyway, you're welcome to come with me to see Mabel."

"I'd like that," Cassie said simply.

22

Mabel was just finishing her supper when Becca and Cassie entered the room. She beamed at them. "Oh, good. You've saved me from eating this green Jell-O—or at least that's what I think it is. Cassie, come give me a hug. What a special treat to have both you and Becca here."

Cassie's eyes filled with tears as she hugged Mabel. "I was so worried when I heard what happened to you, Mrs. Wright. Are you feeling any better?"

Mabel laughed. "Oh, don't worry, I'll live. I'm a tough old bird."

Becca patted Mabel affectionately on the arm. "Al Scott told me you'll be able to go home with him tomorrow."

"And not a moment too soon, the way

they poke and prod me, not to mention the food they serve that even my dog Tex would refuse to eat." Mabel's face softened at the mention of her dog.

Becca laughed. "You sound to me like you're in fine form. Good to see it."

Cassie spoke up. "Mrs. Wright, you've probably already guessed that Mrs. Anderson has taken me into her confidence. May I see the page you showed her the other evening?"

"It's there, child." Mabel pointed to the wooden box on her bedside table. "Go ahead and look at it. I've long suspected that you were one of us. Your mother, God rest her soul, had a very strong power."

Cassie nodded solemnly. She opened the wooden box and retrieved the document. It was so old that she was afraid it might crumble in her hands. "I did some research on my laptop after Mrs. Anderson told me about this, and I think it's a page from an old book on Scottish folklore."

Mabel interjected, "You goggled it, did you? No one seems to rely on books any more."

Cassie bit her lip to keep from smiling. She had no intention of telling Mrs. Wright that the correct word was *googled*. "Well, there's not much on the internet about it, that's for sure. I asked Jenny at the library to put aside some books for me on Scottish history."

Cassie looked at the document and read the account of the slaughtered victims. "Then I guess there's no doubt that the descendants are targeting us for revenge."

She had a sudden thought that made her shudder involuntarily. "We don't even know when these acts of revenge started."

Becca said, "No we don't. This has obviously been planned for centuries. My guess is the story has been passed on from generation to generation to keep the hatred alive."

Cassie replied, "The irony is there's no evidence that the original victims were guilty of any wrongdoing."

23

Wednesday Afternoon/Evening

Al Scott took Mabel's arm and helped her navigate the steps to his house. His wife watched anxiously from the living room window. Once inside, Al led her to an upholstered chair while his wife fussed with the cushions. On cue Tex bounded into the room and jumped up to lick his mistress's face. Mabel hugged him with all her might, the tears streaming down her cheeks. "Good Tex. Good boy," she repeated over and over again.

Al shook his head at his wife as she was about to coax Tex into getting down. "Let them be, Doreen," he said. His voice was hoarse.

At supper later that evening, Al cleared his throat, looking as if he was about to say something that had him deeply conflicted. "Mabel, we wanted you to stay with us until you got your strength back. I can't stand the thought of you being in that house alone again."

Mabel spoke up. "I appreciate that, Al. I really do. But what is it that's upsetting you?"

"Well, our son Jason—you probably remember him as a tyke—called last night. It seems he's been planning a surprise for me now that I'm retired. He bought airplane tickets for Doreen and me to go to Arizona. He's rented a condominium there for us."

"But Al, that's wonderful news. When are the two of you leaving?"

"That's just it, Mabel. We don't want to leave you alone—"

"Nonsense, Al. There're other places I can stay. I'm sure Becca Anderson would be happy to put me up."

"But she has a cat. Tex isn't going to like that much."

"Well, I've been thinking of leaving Tex with my sister Jane for a couple of weeks, anyway. Just until I get up to snuff."

Al Scott still looked unhappy, as did his wife who was bustling back and forth clearing dishes and trying to keep tabs on the conversation at the same time.

"Tell you what, Al. Give Becca a call right now and see if there's any problem with my going there. I don't expect there will be."

24

Becca was jumpy. When the phone rang, she thought she'd catapult right out of her chair. "Yes, yes, hello." She listened to Al Scott at the other end of the line, heaving a sigh of relief that it was not the Harris boy calling to warn her that the enemy was coming.

Get a grip, she told herself, trying to concentrate on what Al was saying.

"No, Al, that won't be a problem at all. In fact, Cassie Patterson is staying with me right now, and I've still got lots of room. We'd love to have Mabel here. When did you say you were leaving?"

"Well, my son's scheduled a taxi to take us to the airport bright and early tomorrow morning," he said reluctantly.

"That's not a problem. You can leave Tex at Jane's house and then bring Mabel here. We'll be waiting for her. I'll get her bed ready."

******

Al Scott had dropped Tex off, but he was still worried.

Who's going to keep the driveways open when I'm gone? And who's going to keep the rink up?

But another part of him felt inexplicably relieved that he and his wife were leaving Berwick Street.

******

Al helped Mabel into the Anderson house, waited until she was settled in, and then brought her suitcase from his truck.

Becca said, "Have a good trip, Al, and enjoy the warmth. I'm glad you're getting out before the next storm hits."

"Are you sure you ladies will be okay? What about the snowplowing? Who's going to keep your driveway clear?"

"Al, don't worry about that. Cassie's already made a few calls and she's lined up someone to do that. We've got lots of food on hand, and I've arranged with Merrill Jonsson to rent a generator in case we lose the power again. Go on now, and enjoy yourself. I think that's supposed to be the point of retirement," she teased as she shooed him out the door.

Once the door was closed and Becca could hear the sound of Al's old truck starting, she turned to Mabel. "Okay, give, Mabel. Did you engineer all of this?"

Cassie entered from the kitchen. "Actually, I did, Mrs. Anderson. I called Jason—remember we went to school together?—and suggested that his dad was wearing himself out with all the snow removal and the upkeep on the skating rink. The rest was up to Jason, and he came through admirably. He said he'd already been thinking of coaxing his parents down south and had begun making some serious inquiries. That's how he managed to rent the condo for them on such short notice."

"Thank you, my dear," Mabel said. "I was desperately worried about what might happen to Al and Doreen, and I did so much want to join you two. I'm old, but I can help. My vision's still good, and I can start going through those old books you got from the library to see if they'll help us."

25

Wednesday Evening, 10 PM –
Thursday Morning, 12:30 AM

Under different circumstances, the atmosphere would have been almost festive. The three ladies had changed into their night gowns and robes and were watching an old Cary Grant movie on the Turner Classic Movies channel. Becca had located a bottle of brandy left over from Christmas, and they were all sipping from small glasses of the liquor as they watched the movie.

******

Mabel was now drowsing quietly in her chair, and Becca thought how lonely the woman must be. She'd lived without her husband and children for so many years now. After her hip replacement a couple of years back, Mabel had been able to get out more, but now that her other hip was showing signs of deterioration, she walked with a cane and was a virtual shut-in. Becca knew that she had young volunteers visiting her every week, but she suspected that Mabel missed the company of adults. Her sister Jane lived nearby on a farm but seemed to be constantly working either with the farm animals or the crops and didn't visit that often.

Becca made a mental note that she would make more time for Mabel in the future.

If we have a future.

She shifted her gaze to Cassie, who was still wide-awake and just finishing the last of her drink. She was short and petite—probably not more than 5 feet tall—with straight black hair that fell to her waist.

How intense she always seems. I remember she was like that even as a child. As if she had some special knowledge, and the world was not as bright a place for her as it was for my own children.

******

The two older women had gone to bed. Cassie sat at Becca's dining room table with her Ouija board spread in front of her. She was glad to be alone at the moment because she needed time to think and plan for the ordeal ahead. Tomorrow the three of them would decide how they could go about defending themselves and the other few remaining residents of Berwick Street who had not gone south for the winter.

There was a sudden movement of the planchette on which she rested her fingers. She sensed that it was Dietrich who was communicating with her again this evening.

The message he sent was cryptic:

2 days

Cassie had asked the spirit board how long they had before their enemies launched an all-out attack.

Now she knew how little time they had to prepare.

26

Thursday, 1 AM

The spirit Dietrich was deeply disturbed. He wanted to help Cassie and her friends, but already he could feel his adversaries challenging his strength.

Quickly, quickly now.

With an invisible force, as if a finger were absently tracing the circumference of a globe, he drew a protective circle around the house where Cassie was staying.

This won't last long with the attack coming, but at least it will keep her safe for now.

"Are you here, Edward and Jana? The Guardians are about to attack again. We need to be ready."

The spirit of Edward answered. "I am here, Dietrich, and I'll stand with you. I promised her mother I would protect her."

And then Jana added her voice. "I too have promised her mother to protect her. I'm ready."

27

Thursday, 3 AM

James Sampson sat at an old table, its surface scarred by knife marks and burns. He sensed that Dietrich was doing what he could to protect the young woman. His father had warned him about the spirit: he'd had his own battles with Dietrich and lost. But James was stronger than his father because the strength of each subsequent generation of the Guardians of Truth had grown. And he believed that the influence of Dietrich was waning.

He looked at the clock.

Three AM. The soul's midnight. The point at which the human body is most susceptible to death.

He was not normally given to introspection, but now it was as if a shadow had fallen upon him, and he shook his head sadly.

When did this desire for revenge finally consume my whole life? I had a wife once and a young daughter, and I loved them dearly. But I shut them out, and they left me. It must be at least twenty years since I last saw them.

Did I make the right choice? Did I really have a choice?

He recalled the long hours he'd spent with his grandfather and father as they read to him from the old journals. The Scottish king had gone to claim his bride in Denmark, and a storm at sea had hit their vessel on the return voyage. The storm was blamed on sorcery, and soon two villages and two countries were engulfed in chaos.

They had tortured the young maid Gillis Duncan until she became the accuser, and then no one was safe from the townspeople.

He could almost hear the screams of the victims and smell the burning flesh.

The social scientists pointed to it as an episode of "moral panic," an example of misguided beliefs that made the townspeople think their social order was in jeopardy.

How neat and tidy it must be to categorize such atrocities.

But there was nothing moral about the

slaughter of innocents. About the destruction of his ancestors except for the few who remained to pass on the true story to their sons and daughters.

A solemn legacy born of the need to avenge their forefathers.

And in two days, they would have everything in place and, hopefully, it would go right this time and would all be over.

28

Thursday, 6 AM

Becca was drinking her coffee as she watched out her kitchen window. She saw the taxi turn into the Scotts' driveway.

The driver hurried from his cab and knocked briskly on the front door. It opened, and she saw that he was being handed several heavy suitcases, which he subsequently placed in the trunk of the cab.

She continued to watch as Al and Doreen Scott made their way to the taxi and climbed into the back seat.

Becca heaved a sigh of relief.

At least they've escaped. They're safe for now. That's all we can ask.

29

Thursday, 9 AM

Spurred by Cassie's revelation that they had only two days left before the final assault would begin, the three women were starting their own preparations. Mabel was wearing her reading glasses and going through an old history book on Scotland. Becca was searching through her chest of drawers to locate a necklace she hadn't worn since she was a teenager. Cassie was spreading some objects on the dining room table: candles of various colours, herbs, incense, and an old jewellery box that had once belonged to her mother.

"I found it," Becca exclaimed as she entered the living room, and the other two women looked up expectantly. She was holding a tiny gold cross in her hand. "I'm not sure if this will help a lapsed Protestant but, Cassie, you told us each to find a talisman. I think this is the best I can do."

Cassie nodded. "Good. Then keep it with you all the time now. Don't let it out of your sight. Mrs. Wright, were you able to find something?"

"As much as it will serve an old reprobate, I have this Bible. My mother gave it to me when I was a child. I have a passage marked." Mabel began to read aloud from Psalm 23 in a loud, clear voice: "The Lord is my shepherd ..."

The intensity with which Mabel read the lines touched Cassie, causing her to pause.

I've always loved that passage as well. To be able to believe in an all-powerful being, that must be very special. But it's not possible for me. I'm not a Christian, although I'd never question the right of anyone else to believe in Christ. There have been too many wars fought and too many lives lost when followers of one religion tried to impose their beliefs, like martial law, on others. And looking at this world, I understand why people are comforted by words and symbols of a resurrection and a better life to come.

What do I believe in, exactly? I don't know if I can put a name to it. I believe strongly in a moral order and in the sanctity of nature. That much I know....

"Is everything okay, Cassie?" Becca asked. "You look like you're miles away."

"Oh, yes, sorry. I was thinking of something else. Mrs. Wright, that's an excellent talisman. And it's important to keep reciting those verses in your head until they become a mantra."

Mabel said, "I think I've found something else that can help us." She opened the history book and began to read a passage aloud to them. The other women listened attentively. When she'd finished reading, Mabel put the book aside and waited for their reaction.

Becca spoke first. "If I understand correctly, the whole impetus for this tragedy was a storm at sea. Perhaps they'll use the coming storm against us. They did that before when they tried to poison you, Mabel, and run you down with your car, Cassie."

"I agree," Cassie said. "So we must do our best to neutralize the effects of this storm. When is Mr. Jonsson going to deliver the generator, by the way?"

"It should be here by noon."

"Good. I've got some extra gas cans. I'll get them filled later this morning. Do you mind if I take your car again, Mrs. Anderson, and fill the tank as well? I forgot to do that yesterday when I was buying the groceries. I'm a little wary about using my car again after what happened."

"Yes, by all means take it. And I've got some jerry cans in the garage. We should fill as many as we can find to run the generator."

"Speaking of which, where is Mr. Jonsson going to set it up?" Cassie asked. "We need someplace safe. They've already tried to poison Mrs. Wright with carbon monoxide fumes."

"I've asked him to set it up in the garage: it's detached and the gas fumes can't seep into the house. Back in '98 when we had that horrible ice storm, we almost froze—you remember, Mabel, we spent a lot of time at your house around the wood stove—so afterward my husband Jack had new wiring installed to connect a generator with the furnace and whatever appliances we needed to operate in a storm. He also bought a huge generator, but I gave that one to Elizabeth because she lives out in the country. Hopefully, the generator that Merrill's bringing will still do the trick."

"How are you going to get power from the generator to the house?" Cassie asked.

"When he got the new wiring installed, Jack also bought extra-length extension cords with special fittings that could be plugged into the generator and then run to the house. That's my Jack," Becca smiled absently, "always thinking of everything."

"Okay then. I'm heading out to get the gas. Then I'm going to make the rounds of our neighbours—the ones who haven't headed down south—and see if they need anything before the storm hits." Cassie was making a mental list of those who remained on the street. In addition to the three of them and Edna and Nick Harris, there was Mrs. MacIntyre, a widow with severe asthma who stayed indoors and was on oxygen most of the time. There were Susan and Dan Beckwith and their two teenaged boys, friends of Nick Harris, no doubt. There was also Karen MacDonald, a single mother of two young children, who worked at a local restaurant. Like Cassie, Karen had inherited her house. Otherwise she would never have been able to afford the mortgage.

"While I'm gone, Mrs. Wright, can you continue reading to see if there are any other passages that can help? And please start making a complete list of the victims so we can try to identify their descendants. Maybe we'll find something we can use to exploit their weaknesses." *If they have any.*

"I'll get some other stuff ready while

you're gone," Becca said. "I still have candles I put away for emergencies. I'll round up some more wooden matches, and I'll put new batteries in the flashlights from the packs you bought yesterday. Is there anything I'm forgetting?"

"Do you have an old battery-powered radio?" Cassie asked.

"Yes, I think there's one in the attic."

"Okay. We've got lots of water jugs and plenty of canned goods, including cat food for Mooch, so if you can line up an old-style can opener, that would be good. I'll pick up some plastic sheeting at the hardware store. Can you find some old tarps and a staple gun?" Seeing Becca's questioning look, Cassie said, "I'll explain later how we can use all this stuff.

"Anything else you ladies need me to pick up while I'm out?"

Mabel looked up from her reading. "Well, now that you mention it, I wouldn't mind another bottle of that brandy we had last night. I rather fancied it."

30

Thursday, 1 PM

Mabel was having an afternoon nap, and Cassie was still out getting the last of their provisions and visiting the remaining neighbours.

Becca washed her hands in the bathroom, staring at her reflection in the mirror above the sink. She'd always taken a utilitarian approach to her appearance, keeping her curly hair cut short and her make-up to a minimum.

Leah had given her some anti-aging products for her last birthday, and she'd tried valiantly to stick to the regimen recommended on the packages. One product in particular amused her. It was described as a filler and sealant and had been designed to smooth out wrinkles. Every time Becca put some in the deep smile lines that bracketed her mouth, she felt like a painter plastering over old cracks. After a week or two, she'd put the products away in her bathroom cabinet, hoping Leah wouldn't mind if her mother didn't look new and improved when she saw her next.

Now Becca was examining her wrinkles in the mirror with a sense of defeat.

Who am I, anyway?

At one time, when I was at university in the '70s, I thought of myself as a feminist, but I never really was accepted by that group. I remember how I inwardly cringed every time that professor of women's studies— what was her name, oh yes, Maureen Barker—read from The Female Eunuch *and denounced women who wore makeup as objectifying themselves (but was there truly anything wrong with trying to feel attractive, not for men, but for yourself?), women who didn't want to work, who wanted only the* institutions *of marriage and family, making them sound like the modern equivalent of slavery.*

But then after I married Jack and we decided to have the children (and admit it, Rebecca, you still felt guilty because you could hear Professor Barker's voice in your head lecturing you on the traps of marriage and motherhood), I was so busy that I kind of lost sight of myself.

And when Elizabeth was in high school and Leah and Jim were at university and I went back to work, it was like I had missed it all, even though I was only in my mid-forties. The young women—they seemed so impossibly self-assured—treated me like a relic of the old days, and the few older women, who had been widowed or divorced, couldn't understand why I was working when I had a perfectly good husband and breadwinner.

And here I sit in this house, and I'm still someone's mother and now someone's grandmother. These are roles. Granted, they're ones I love and happily fulfill, but there's got to be more to me than this.

I've automatically deferred to a woman who's less than half my age and let her assume the leadership.

But this is too important, dammit.

Time to step up to the plate, Rebecca. There's no room for self-doubts any more.

Pull yourself together. First thing to do is call the children so they won't worry if they can't get you.

And say good-bye to them, if that's how this must end.

31

Thursday, 1:30 PM

Elizabeth Anderson, the youngest of Becca's children, was sitting at her drawing table, sketching a design for a logo commissioned by an Ottawa business. She worked from home, which was a century-old stone house that she and her partner, Julia Simmons, had purchased on the outskirts of a small village about forty-five minutes from Ottawa. Julia also had an office in their new home, but was rarely there during the day. She worked as a large-animal vet and spent most of her time visiting the local farms and stables to tend to sick cattle, horses, goats, and sheep or to assist in difficult births. The two of them had met in the last year of high school and had been together ever since.

Lost in thought, Elizabeth was startled

by the ringing of her cellphone. She saw from the caller ID that it was her mother.

"Mom, this is a nice surprise. I don't often hear from you during the day. What's up?"

"Just calling to let you know there's another big storm coming and to see if the old generator's working okay."

Elizabeth laughed. "I never keep track of those things, Mom, but I'm sure Julia's got it primed and ready to go. You know how practical she is compared to me.

"What about you, Mom? You okay in case you get snowed in?"

"I'm fine here. Actually, I've got a couple of house guests to keep me company." Becca was deliberately vague about why the two women were staying with her, but Elizabeth didn't seem to notice. "Anyway, I just wanted to let you know—in case the power and telephone lines go out—that I'll be doing okay. I love you, Elizabeth."

"Love you too, Mom."

******

Jim Anderson was sitting at his desk in his Ottawa office, reviewing his notes for a court appearance. He was an energetic man who seldom slept more than five hours a night. As a defence attorney, he'd worked his way up from defending clients charged with minor drug offences to major criminal cases. He was the senior partner in his own law firm and always carried a heavy workload, but he still did a lot of pro bono work for those too poor to pay his fees.

One case in particular still haunted him. He had just started his practice and was defending a young man who'd suffered chronic physical and sexual abuse in a boys' school in nearby Alfred, Ontario. Just out of his teens, the young man had turned to alcohol and drugs to deal with his depression, committing a string of petty thefts to support his habit. The judge had impatiently waved aside the brief Jim had carefully prepared with details of the abuse as mitigating circumstances in the sentencing phase and had given the young man a lengthy prison term. While awaiting transfer from the regional detention centre to a federal penitentiary, the young man hanged himself in his cell.

Jim was thinking of that case now as he read his notes on the young offender he was currently representing. He looked up as his secretary appeared at his office door.

"Excuse me, Jim, but your mom's on the line and I thought you might want to take the call."

"Yes, thanks, you can put her through."

"Sorry to bother you, Jim, during the day when I know you're very busy but we're getting hit by another major storm, and I didn't want you to worry if you couldn't reach me. I've got lots of extras, and I rented a generator so Mooch and I are all set. I hope you don't get too much snow in Ottawa. I know they're a bit slow there plowing out the streets."

"Well, if I need to, I can always walk to work. I'm glad to hear that you're doing okay though. I'll be down soon to pay you a visit. It's been a while, hasn't it? I sure miss your cooking! You spoiled me at Christmas. Last time I tried to cook a turkey myself, I ended up stapling it shut to keep the stuffing in. That went over really well with my guests, I'll tell you."

Becca laughed and then turned serious. "I love you, Jim, and I'm very proud of you, son."

"I love you too, Mom. See you soon."

******

Becca left the most difficult call to the end. She'd never been able to mask her feelings from her oldest daughter. Somehow, Leah always knew when her mother was upset.

With the three-hour time difference, Becca expected Leah would still be teaching a class and had planned to leave her a message, so she was surprised when her daughter answered the phone.

"Oh, Leah, I thought I'd get your voice mail. I hope I'm not interrupting you in class."

"No, Mom. I just have early morning classes on Thursday. I'm finished for the day. Everything okay there?"

"Yes, just wanted to check to see if you and Charlotte are still planning to come in March for the spring break."

"We wouldn't miss it, Mom. That's all Charlotte talks about. We've already got our plane tickets."

"Wonderful! Oh, and I wanted to let you know that I'm all set for the next storm in case you hear about it on the weather channel. I know you were concerned about me the last time." She told Leah that Cassie and Mabel were staying with her and not to worry.

"Odd that Mabel would leave her house when she's got that wood stove in case the power goes out."

"Well, as I said, I've rented a generator, and I thought Mabel would be cosy here. She doesn't get around as well as she used to. Her dog Tex is staying with her sister. We agreed that Mooch wouldn't appreciate doggie company."

"Are you still having those ... bad feelings, Mom? As if something's going to happen?"

Becca crossed her fingers and tried not to feel guilty about lying to her daughter. "No, they're gone. I think maybe I was just worried about Mabel. That's why I asked her to stay with me. Someone's at the door, Leah," she fibbed, "so I need to go. Love you. Give Charlotte a big, big hug for me."

"Love you too, Mom. Don't you ladies have too many late nights, now. Talk to you soon."

32

Mabel was still napping, but now she had started to dream. She was in the front passenger seat of a vehicle—she didn't know who was driving—when the road suddenly ended and she was standing on a bridge. To her left was a luscious field, and she watched as wild animals walked slowly—two by two—through the tall grass.

She looked up suddenly and saw children with angel wings flying overhead. Her rational mind told her this was impossible, but in dream logic the children continued to float peacefully above her.

Suddenly two of the children turned toward her, and she could see their faces. It was Anthony and Nicholas, her long-lost twins.

When she awoke, her face was wet with tears.

Buck up, Mabel. It was just a dream. That's what her mother would have told her—her mother who'd been a true Victorian in every sense of the word and who'd always been mortified by any show of emotion. *Buck up.*

But still Mabel wept for her lost sons.

33

Thursday, 2:30 PM

Becca was assembling the last of the material that Cassie had requested, as well as adding a few items of her own. She was hesitating now in the kitchen, finally reaching far back into the cupboard to extract an old box bound with twine. The box contained a bone-handled carving set that had been a wedding gift for her and Jack.

I was always terrified the kids might cut themselves on these knives. Jack kept them razor-sharp even though he only used them two or three times a year.

But would I ever have the nerve to use them?

She hesitated, then took the box and placed it under her reading chair in the living room, which was beginning to resemble a hardware store.

She saw that Mabel had finished her nap and was busy at work again going through the old books and making notes. Mabel looked up as Becca entered the living room. "I see you've been busy while I was napping." Mabel pointed to all the items assembled on the floor. "I've got that list Cassie asked for. You know, the list of victims."

"Thanks, Mabel. I'm going to work the rest of the afternoon on my computer and see if I can locate their descendants. It's amazing the amount of information that's available. There's one Scottish genealogy site I've already scoped out that can trace ancestors back to 1513."

Mabel shook her head. "I'll leave you to it then. I'm sticking with these books."

For the rest of the afternoon, the two women worked in silence, well aware that time was running out for them.

34

Thursday, 3 PM

Cassie had made her neighbourhood rounds except for the Harrises, whom she'd left for last. She'd been relieved to discover that Mrs. MacIntyre, the shut-in, had her niece staying with her, who had already ordered extra tanks of oxygen for her aunt, as well as purchasing additional groceries. She seemed to have things well in hand. The other neighbours were prepared as well for the second wave of the storm, but thanked Cassie for checking in on them.

Edna Harris was just getting out of her car when Cassie arrived at her house.

"Hi, Cassie. Good to see you. I just finished work. Come on in."

Cassie helped her carry groceries from the car. "I'm glad to see you had a chance to stock up."

"Yes, I guess this storm's got everyone nervous after the last dump of snow we got," Edna said as Cassie followed her to the kitchen and placed the bags she was carrying on the counter.

Nick was having a snack at the table, his crutches propped against a chair. "Hi, Miss Patterson."

"Hi, Nick. I just stopped by to see if you and your mom needed anything, but it looks like your mom already has that covered. How much longer will you need to wear that?" Cassie pointed to his cast.

"At least another two weeks," he said glumly.

Cassie gave him a commiserating look and then turned to his mother. "Mrs. Wright and I are staying with Becca Anderson for a while."

Edna looked surprised, but didn't say anything.

"I'll leave you my cellphone number in case there's anything you need. I'd be happy to get it for you."

Edna thanked her and, looking at her son, said, "It may be a bit boring for Nick if school's cancelled again, but he'll find other stuff to keep him busy." She ruffled his hair affectionately.

Looking embarrassed, Nick rolled his eyes at Cassie. "My mom thinks I spend too much time on the internet."

Both women laughed.

"Would you like a cup of tea or coffee, Cassie?" Edna offered.

"Thanks, but I told Mrs. Anderson I'd be home in time to help her with supper. Take care, you two," Cassie said as she prepared to leave. She glanced over at Nick and, seeing the troubled look that had come into his eyes, patted his arm for reassurance.

35

Thursday, 7–9 PM

After a quick supper, the three women began to prepare the house against an assault. It was a ranch-style bungalow with bedrooms on the main floor level. Cassie and Becca stapled plastic sheeting to each of the windows. Cassie had also placed small bags of anise in each window, a herb used as protection against negative forces, she explained to the other two women.

"This heavy plastic will at least cut down on the amount of flying glass if they break the windows.

"I'm going outside now to move the gasoline cans to the garage. I'll fill the generator and then connect the power cords. I can use the tarps you found, Mrs. Anderson, to cover the cords and protect them from the snow."

"I'll go out with you and help. Mabel's fine here. She's still writing out the list."

Cassie and Becca spent an hour outside getting everything ready. They were chilled to the bone when they finally came inside the house.

"How's the list coming, Mrs. Wright?" Cassie asked.

"It's done." Mabel handed the list of names to Cassie, who couldn't help but admire the beautiful cursive script in which it had been written. Mabel and Becca had come through for Cassie, identifying the modern descendants of the original victims. In all, they were facing at least nine adversaries.

Cassie added text at the bottom of the sheet—the wording of a white magic spell to cast out evil—photocopied it on Becca's printer, and then inserted each of the copies in plastic protective sleeves that Becca had found in some old school supplies. Cassie used a staple gun to fasten the lists to the front and back wooden doors of the house.

"I still don't understand how that list will help us," Becca said.

"It may not," Cassie admitted, "but the descendants can trace their lineage back several centuries, and I'm relying on the ancient belief that knowing someone's true name gives you power over that person. Naming has always been an important element of white magic for protection against the dark arts. And also, it will come as a complete surprise to them to see their names because I suspect that up to now they've operated in anonymity. I'm hoping the list will make them pause and give us a chance to arm ourselves before they attack. I don't expect that we'll have the strength to fight them off physically, but I'm hoping to at least slow them down until my protectors can help us."

Becca looked puzzled. "What are you talking about, Cassie? What protectors?"

Cassie led the other two women to the dining room table where her Ouija board was spread out and asked them to sit with her. "The protectors are spirits I summon through the board," she explained.

"But I thought the Ouija board was supposed to summon up *evil* spirits," Mabel said, reluctantly sitting and placing her fingers on the pointer as Cassie was now instructing her to do.

"That's a common misconception, but the board itself isn't inherently good or evil. It's how the summoner uses it. I've used it to contact benign spirits of the departed— those who haven't yet passed over to the other world. Bear with me, please. I know you're both very skeptical but try to open your minds. If ever there was a time for the willing suspension of disbelief, this is it."

The other women remained silent as Cassie attempted to summon Dietrich, Edward, and Jana.

Slowly the planchette started moving.

We are here. The power of 3.

"What does that message mean?" Becca asked after they'd left the table.

Cassie explained, "Three is a sacred, or at least a very important, number in many religions." She pointed to the Bible that Mabel was now clutching in her hands. "There are almost five hundred references to the number three in the Bible. The three patriarchs, the Three Wise Men, the three days of Christ's resurrection, to name only a few examples.

"In Buddhism there are the Three Jewels: the Buddha, the Dhamma, which is the path to enlightenment based on the teachings of Buddha, and the Sangha, the community of the enlightened.

"In Jewish tradition, the number three in the Torah is the number of truth and reconciliation.

"In Taoism, three represents the Great Triad of heaven, human, and earth.

"The number three is also central to modern practitioners of white magic referred to as Wiccans. For example, incantations are always repeated three times, and many of the followers of Wicca believe in the Rule of Three—that the energy one puts forth in the world, whether it be positive or negative, will return threefold to that person."

"Where did you learn all of this, Cassie?" Becca asked.

The young woman blushed. "Sorry, I didn't mean to ramble on. It's just that I rarely have the chance to discuss subjects that interest me. Since my mother died, I've spent a lot of time studying different religions. Despite all the blood that's been shed in their name, they share many similar beliefs. The belief in the Golden Rule, for example, is part of both the Wiccan religion and Christianity."

Mabel, who'd been listening but had said nothing up to this point, interjected, "So perhaps it's good that there are three of us fighting this evil."

Cassie nodded, not wanting to tell her that if there were nine descendants who were their enemies, they would have three times the power.

36

Thursday, nearing midnight—First Watch

From now on, the three women would take alternating eight-hour shifts to watch for the approach of their enemies. Becca had offered to take the first shift—Cassie had noticed a new boldness and sense of purpose in the older woman and was grateful for it—but Cassie wasn't tired and said she would take it.

Now she sat at the dining room table listening to the tune from her mother's old jewellery box. The melody, "Lara's Theme" from *Doctor Zhivago*, began playing as soon as the box was opened. There was also a small ballerina who twirled in time to the music, but the box was so old that the mechanism for the ballerina had stopped working.

One of the saddest, yet most beautiful pieces of music ever written. Lost love. Like ours, Mom. I miss you so much. I wish you were here now to help me.

Cassie unwrapped her own talisman, a brooch that had once belonged to her mother. It was a beautiful, jewel-encrusted pentagram, the star pointing upward to heaven. A long-sacred symbol for many religions.

She knew the symbol had been perverted by Satanists into the Sigil of Baphomet, the official logo of the Church of Satan with two points upward, a double circle around the star, and the head of a goat inside the pentagram.

The overhead chandelier turned the bejewelled brooch into a dazzling prism of colours. Fascinated by the display, Cassie accidentally bumped the jewellery box with her elbow and sent it crashing to the floor.

Oh no, what have I done?

She hurriedly picked up the box and surveyed the damage. The bottom drawer was loose and, as she pulled on it, she discovered a hidden compartment. There was a small leather-bound notebook inside.

She opened it and read the inscription on the flyleaf: "To my beloved Cassandra."

This is no coincidence. I asked my mother

for help and she's given me this.

Cassie began to read the journal:

I have hidden this book from your father because he was never comfortable with my beliefs. If you're grown up now, Cassandra, then you've probably realized from what I taught you as a young child that I am a Wiccan and believe in the sanctity of all life.

In spite of our detractors, many of whom believe we worship Satan, there is a strong morality at the heart of the Wiccan religion. I believe in the Wiccan Rede:

An' it harm none, do
what thou wilt.

I tell you this because I want you to know that I took steps to protect myself from the worshippers of Satan, but I failed. As I am writing this, I am slowly dying....

Evil never dies, Cassandra, it merely transmutes into other forms. I believe that you too are in danger as my offspring. After I die, I'll make certain you have protectors to look after you.

And now I will explain to you the nature of the evil that you must battle as I tried to battle it before you...

37

Friday Morning, nearing 8:00 AM—Second Watch

Becca was sitting at the dining room table with Cassie, about to relieve her of her watch. "Can I make you some breakfast, Cassie, before you go to sleep?"

"No, thanks anyway, I'll get something later." She showed Becca the notebook she'd found. "I'm only about half-way through it, but I've already learned a lot. It's as we suspected: this has been going on for centuries. And, apparently, our precognitive abilities are no accident. These powers developed over time with each successive generation of our families in order to counter those of the victims' descendants."

Becca said, "Since this whole thing started, I've felt guilty. You know, for what our ancestors did to those poor people—"

"You mustn't feel that way, Mrs. Anderson. What our ancestors did was horrible, but we are in no way to blame for their actions. And this group has killed thousands of innocent people since that time, my own mother among them. She wrote most of this journal when she knew she was dying. Look at this passage."

Becca read from the notebook Cassie handed her and then looked up in shock. "They poisoned her? Oh, Cassie, I'm so sorry."

38

Friday, 4 PM—Third Watch

Mabel had prepared a light snack for herself and Becca, before taking over the watch. She hadn't slept well because she'd had a nagging feeling that she wasn't alone. When she woke up, Mooch the cat was lying on her bed, staring at her with his huge green eyes, and it had unnerved her.

Becca noticed that Mabel was having more difficulty than usual getting around. "Are you okay, Mabel?"

"I'm fine. It's just the snow coming. The damp air always makes my hip throb. I can forecast weather better than any of those blasted meteorologists. What have you got there?" Mabel pointed to the notebook in Becca's hands.

"It's a journal Cassie found. Her mother

wrote it before her death. Apparently she died from a slow-acting poison." Becca showed her the relevant passage from the notebook.

Mabel shuddered. "God, I wonder how many deaths were at the hands of our adversaries."

"We don't really know, Mabel, and maybe we'll never know. We need to concentrate on the present so we can prevent any further deaths. Do you feel up to taking the third watch?"

"Of course. I'll just keep moving around so my hip doesn't stiffen up on me." And then, assuming a bravado she did not feel, Mabel said, "Besides, according to our young friend Cassie, the number three is good. Go on now and get some sleep, Becca. You look exhausted."

******

Mabel watched as the storm began, and snow pelted the windows of the Anderson house.

The Lord is my shepherd, I shall not want. The Lord is my shepherd, I shall not want.

Cassie told me to repeat it like a mantra.

It's been so long since I've been in church. I mostly lost my faith when the twins and then Bruce died. I'm not sure if my prayers will mean anything.

If it's my time, so be it.

And then she began to chant her mantra once again.

39

Friday, Midnight—Fourth Watch

Cassie had taken over from Mabel, who hugged her before leaving to get some sleep.

Outside the storm was whipping up to a frenzy, but they hadn't lost power—yet.

Cassie turned on the radio. There were numerous road closures and no end in sight to the storm. She turned it off again, not needing any further bad news.

Two days. Forty-eight hours. The attack is imminent.

She fingered her mother's pentagram brooch and continued to read from the journal:

> You are probably just beginning
> to realize the extent of your powers,

Cassandra, and they will strengthen with use. I saw them in you even when you were just a little girl. With practice you will be able to control objects with your mind....

Suddenly the lights flickered and the power went off.

Cassie lit some candles and put on her coat. She grabbed a flashlight and then stepped outside into the blizzard to start the generator.

When she returned, she saw that Mooch was on the table. "Shoo, Mooch, you're not supposed to be up there."

The cat raised his back and hissed at her. When it jumped down from the table, it knocked her mother's brooch to the floor.

Cassie knelt to pick it up.

It felt warm to the touch.

40

Saturday Morning, 2 AM

"Can you see them, Roland?" asked James Sampson of his friend as the two of them sat in the meeting place awaiting the arrival of the other members of the group.

"Yes, I've taken the body of the cat as a familiar. They're rotating watches now, and it appears that the young one has found a notebook from her mother."

Sampson sneered, "It's a bit too late for that, don't you think? Besides, her mother was powerless against us in the end."

Roland appeared unsettled as he said, "Do you ever question any of this, James? I mean, whether we have the moral right to kill people who are innocent of any wrongdoing?"

After a long hesitation Sampson replied,

"I'll admit that I've experienced my own doubts lately. But in my heart I believe we are more sinned against than sinning. I think, no matter what happens, we're committed to playing out this final act."

Sampson then called upon the powers of the Ancient Ones. "Lucifer, Azazel, Belial ... lead us into victory."

41

Friday, nearing midnight (Pacific Time); nearing 3 AM (Eastern Time)

Leah had managed to get Charlotte to cuddle up next to one of her favourite teddy bears and fall asleep around 8 PM.

Now she was sitting on her couch, sipping a glass of wine and reading a book. It was a luxury for her to have this time to herself to relax. It didn't happen very often.

The quiet was interrupted by a scream from Charlotte that sent chills down Leah's back.

She rushed into her daughter's bedroom. Charlotte was awake and crying hysterically.

"Mommy, mommy, the bad people are coming for Grandma. Please help her. They'll kill her. They will. Just like they killed the

Christmas spirit. Grandma knows who they are and she's trying very hard to be brave, but she needs our help."

Leah tried to comfort her daughter, but she was inconsolable. Finally, she said, "I know what we can do, Charlotte. If I can't reach Grandma on the phone, I'll call your Aunt Elizabeth and she can check on Grandma. Would that be okay?"

Charlotte finally calmed down a bit. "Okay, Mommy, but hurry."

42

Saturday Morning, nearing 3 AM

Becca startled awake and groped for the ringing phone beside her bed.

"Hello, who's this?"

"Mrs. Anderson, it's Nick. They're coming now. Is there anything I can do to help you?"

"Thank you, Nick. You've already done enough by warning me. I want you to stay where you are and protect yourself and your mom."

Becca rushed to tell Cassie of Nick's warning and to wake Mabel.

Cassie fumbled with the objects on the dining room table, then found some matches and lit three candles. The other two women joined her at the table. She lit one white candle for positive energy, one black for negative energy, and one green to represent the spirit, and repeated a white magic spell to cleanse them of negative energy in preparation for the battle to come.

Suddenly, one of the candles tipped over as if of its own volition, and the tablecloth erupted in flames. Becca raced to get the fire extinguisher from the kitchen to douse the flames.

Objects began to spontaneously combust throughout the living room, and the battery-operated smoke alarms set up a plaintive wail.

Concentrate, Cassie told herself. *Mom said I have the power to control things with my mind.*

With all her strength, she willed the flames to subside. At first nothing happened, and then very slowly the fires were extinguished.

There was an eerie silence in the house as the smoke alarms were suddenly muted.

Outside the only sound was the wind.

The Guardians of Truth prepared for another assault.

43

Saturday Morning, 4 AM

There was a violent sound as the glass in the windows of the Anderson house imploded. The plastic sheeting contained some of the damage, but there were still glass shards everywhere in the house.

Almost mesmerized by the sight, the three women watched as objects suddenly began to take flight.

"Get down," Cassie commanded and each of them sought refuge on the floor.

Mabel chanted, "The Lord is my shepherd."

Becca fingered her gold cross.

Cassie reached up to the dining room table to find her mother's brooch, intoning again and again: "Let this darkness be dispelled, and the power of nature triumph.

Dietrich, Edward, Jana, help us now. Help us now."

But there was no reply.

"Quick, listen. I have a funny story," Cassie said suddenly.

Becca and Mabel looked at the young woman as if she'd lost her mind. Becca said, "I don't think it's the time—"

"No, work with me on this. Laughter lessens their power over us. They hate to be ridiculed."

Cassie began to tell her story. "I was at university. Christmas exams were over, and my roommate talked me into going to the local tavern to celebrate. We both drank too much, and we decided to race back to our apartment. It was bitter cold, but the air felt so good on our faces. I slipped on the ice and fell, and then my roommate lost her footing and fell on top of me. There was a man out walking his dogs, and suddenly this huge Golden Retriever and this miniature poodle came trotting toward us, and the man started calling indignantly, 'Mutt, Jeff, come here right now,' as if he thought we might corrupt his dogs. And my roommate and I rolled on the ice and laughed and laughed until we were out of breath at the sheer absurdity of the situation."

Mabel spoke up. "Well, those are hardly

dignified names for dogs. Tex is a much better name."

And then the three of them looked at each other and began to laugh until tears streamed down their cheeks.

44

Saturday Morning, 4:30 AM

James Sampson's voice rose to a feverish pitch. "They dare laugh at us? Roland, take the others and break down the door."

His second-in-command summoned Angus and Donald. As Roland stood before the door, his flashlight played on the list. He blanched.

"James, our names are here. They know who we are."

"It doesn't matter if they know who we are, Roland. They'll be dead soon enough. Tell the others not to look at the names. It will only weaken them. I'm going back to our meeting place to make sure Dietrich and the others stay away from this house. I leave it to you, Roland, to finish them off. You're in charge."

Roland ordered the younger men to stand guard around the house in case one of the neighbours, drawn by the noise of the smoke detectors and imploding glass, came to investigate. He told Scott Napier to supervise the younger men and to be ready to use his power of pyrokinesis to burn the house to the ground once the women had been killed. Roland then smashed through the door, his eyes avoiding the list, and beckoned Angus Motts and Donald Grierson to follow.

The women were sitting quietly at a table, holding hands, heads bowed. They were chanting, but he could not make out the words.

Roland issued orders to the other two men. "Let's separate them. Angus, use your power of suggestion. Get the old one into the kitchen and the other one into the living room. We'll deal with the young one here."

Roland looked at Cassie as she sat fingering her talisman. "That won't help you now any more than it helped your mother."

45

Mabel felt herself being drawn toward the kitchen. She tried hard to resist, but the force was too strong.

Angus scoffed at her. "You should have died long ago with your sons and husband. The whole worthless lot of you."

"You ... you killed them? How?"

"The power of suggestion, old lady. I can be very persuasive. Your sons were more than happy to go out on that railway bridge. I simply implanted the suggestion in their minds after I'd loosened some of the old boards so they would fall to their death. And your poor, sick husband—well—that was a piece of cake. I removed his nitroglycerine pills from his bedside stand. He didn't have a chance when he had that sudden heart attack. And you're next." He grabbed for her.

Mabel thought, *The dream I had. Being on the bridge. The boys with angel wings. But it was no accident. They were murdered. And Bruce could have survived if he'd had his medication.*

Shaking herself from her stupor, she desperately searched for a weapon, but it was too late. The shock had been too much. Her heart had already been weakened by the carbon monoxide poisoning.

She fell unseeing to the floor.

46

Cassie was fighting them as best she could, still calling desperately on the protection of Dietrich, Edward, and Jana.

"They can't help you now," Donald Grierson said. He used his power of telekinesis to draw glass shards closer toward him. "Any last words?"

The shards suddenly flew into the air toward Cassie, who only had time to raise her hands in an ineffectual effort to deflect them.

For the moment the three men were concentrating on Cassie and Mabel and had left Becca unguarded. She fought desperately against the power exerted over her mind, fingering her cross and willing herself to help Cassie.

She reached under her chair and withdrew the set of bone-handled knives.

God help me.

And then she lunged at Cassie's attacker with one of the knives.

Surprised, Grierson had only enough time to use his power to send a heavy glass vase flying toward Becca's head. She slumped to the floor.

But she had already succeeded in severing the carotid artery in his neck.

47

Saturday Morning, 5 AM

James Sampson had returned to the abandoned shelter. With the help of his demon leaders, he had managed to confuse Cassie's protectors into believing that the women were safe by planting false images in their minds. But gradually the effects of the spell were wearing off.

Sampson sensed the presence of Dietrich and began to ridicule him. "So the great protector is here, but where are your charges? Probably dead as we speak. And what of you, Dietrich, you traitor? You were put to death in your own country for crimes you didn't commit. You could have joined us, you know. But instead you chose the wrong side. You chose to protect the persecutors."

"I tried to tell them that their ways were

wrong, but they wouldn't listen," Dietrich replied. "They were blinded by ignorance and fear. But unlike you, I chose to forgive them and to absolve their descendants of any blame."

"You're a blind fool, Dietrich, and always will be. Unable to recognize your own enemies."

Locked in his hatred, Sampson had been focusing only on Dietrich and did not sense the presence of the other two protectors. Edward and Jana suddenly joined forces with Dietrich.

"You were saying, Sampson? Do you recognize *your* enemies now? Then feel our wrath!"

And Dietrich plunged a sword deep into Sampson's chest.

48

Saturday Morning, 5:15 AM

"Hurry," Dietrich said. "We need to get back to Cassie. We need to protect her and the other women."

When the spirits gathered at the Anderson house, they saw the three women lying lifeless. Enraged, Dietrich threw Angus against a wall. His head slammed backward. He slid down the wall and slumped against the floor, his neck broken.

Recognizing that he could not fight alone against the three spirits, Roland fled the house.

"Quick, come help me," he ordered the men who had been stationed outside the house. Scott Napier immediately came to his side.

The young Thompson spoke first. "Where

are Donald and Angus? Why aren't they here to fight with us?"

"They're both dead," Roland said.

A stunned silence followed. Then Thompson spoke again. "And what can you expect from us when two of our strongest are dead?"

"I expect you to fight alongside me and Scott." Roland suddenly felt the presence of Dietrich and the other two spirits who lifted his body and Napier's into the air and sent them crashing to the ground. Protected by the snow, Roland was dazed but still alive. Napier was not so lucky. His head hit the concrete steps of the house, and his crumpled body lay unmoving on the ground.

There was a frightened murmur among the young ones. Roland stood up and tried to reassure them. "There are still five of us left to fight on. We need to regroup. Let's go back to our meeting place. James is there waiting for us."

It was Thompson again. "Oh yes, and why isn't he here with us when we need him most?"

"It's not your place to question his decisions. And besides, he was leading that woman's protectors astray so they wouldn't intervene. Something must have gone wrong because they were able to reach this house."

"And now three of his own men are dead," Thompson shouted, "and Sampson wasn't even here. I've had enough of this. I'm leaving. Is anyone coming with me? Does anyone else have the guts to stand up to Sampson?"

One of the others spoke up. "He'll slaughter us, Thompson. Just like he killed the two members of our group that dared speak out against him."

"Are we supposed to live the rest of our lives in fear, then? So be it. It's still a better life than pandering to that fanatic. I ask again, is there anyone who'll stand with me?"

Roland tried desperately to intervene, but it was too late. The others joined Thompson and with a final ironic salute to Roland, they fled into the darkness.

Roland stood alone, expecting to meet his death.

But Dietrich said to the other two spirits, "Let him go. He can bear witness to what's become of his great leader. We must see if there's anything that can be done for the women."

49

James Sampson knew he was dying. He'd been complacent, had let down his guard, so sure had he been of victory. And, what irony, he would die at the hands of Dietrich, as had his father before him. He had wanted to die a hero's death, but even that would be denied him.

In the end, was all this really worth it?

The sound of the rusty hinges of the barn door startled him. Someone was coming. Perhaps it was Dietrich to make certain he was dead. Well, he wouldn't have long to wait.

But it was Roland, who now rushed to his side.

Roland grabbed some rags and tried to staunch the flow of blood. "What happened to you, James? What happened?"

"It doesn't matter, now that you're here. You'll take my place with the others once I'm gone. Do you have good news for me?"

Roland eyed his dying friend, recognizing there was nothing more he could do for him. Except, perhaps, one last thing. "The women are dead, James, and our men are making a sweep of the street to destroy anyone who remains. Then we'll hunt down the rest and their children and grandchildren until there are no more survivors. Just like you planned it, James."

And Roland waited with his friend until he died quietly in his arms. Then he went to retrieve the bodies of the other slain Guardians.

50

Saturday Morning, 3-6 AM

Leah had finally called her sister Elizabeth after being unable to reach her mother. With the three-hour time difference, Elizabeth had been fast asleep, but woke up quickly when she heard Leah's voice on the line explaining that Charlotte was frantic about her grandmother.

Elizabeth had tried to reassure her sister that the telephone lines were probably down because of the storm, but Leah still sounded extremely worried. "Mom's been having those 'feelings' again—that something bad was about to happen. She called me on Thursday to tell me not to worry if I couldn't get in touch with her. Mom said everything was okay, but I don't really think she was telling me the truth."

Elizabeth replied, "Funny, she called me too and said the same thing. Tell you what, Julia's on a late-night call, but as soon as she's back with the truck, I'll go see Mom to make sure she's okay."

Leah heaved a sigh of relief. "I owe you one, kiddo. I'll go back and try to calm Charlotte down."

While she waited for Julia to return with the truck, Elizabeth kept calling and calling her mother, but no one was answering. She had been patronizingly reassured by the person who responded to the 1-800 customer service number at the telephone company that her mother's line was open.

Where are you, Mom? Why doesn't someone pick up the damn phone?

Julia had returned home around 5:30 AM, and after a hurried explanation, Elizabeth jumped in the truck and headed for her mother's house. The roads were barely passable with the storm. Driving too fast for the road conditions, she slid around a corner, almost veering off the road until the vehicle's traction control kicked in.

She told herself to slow down. There was probably a logical explanation for all of this. But she was badly frightened.

I pray nothing's happened to her. She's always been there for us, offering advice but never trying to make our decisions for us. When Leah announced she was pregnant and had decided to raise the child as a single mother, Mom never questioned her decision, asking only how she could help out. And Mom has always supported my relationship with Julia, making her feel like one of the family.

It was nearing 6 AM when Elizabeth finally arrived at Berwick Street. Her mother's car was in the driveway, and there were no lights on in the house so she grabbed her flashlight from the truck and raced up the driveway. The front windows had been smashed, and there was broken glass everywhere.

On the front door, Elizabeth's flashlight illuminated a list of names with some mumbo jumbo written underneath about defeating the forces of evil.

What the hell is going on here?

She reached for her house key, but then realized that the lock had already been broken. Her hands were shaking as she opened the door.

The house was bitter cold. There was more broken glass in the hallway and as she shone the light around the living room, Elizabeth saw that the furniture had all been upended. There was a trail of blood on the floor. She spotted her mother lying near an overturned chair and rushed to her side.

"Oh, thank God, Elizabeth. My head is bleeding—they hit me with something heavy—but I'm okay."

Elizabeth punched in 911 on her cellphone. "Mom, what in God's name happened here?"

"I don't have time to explain. Find the others. Go. Find Mabel and Cassie."

Elizabeth reluctantly left her mother's side and began searching the house for the other two women. She found Mabel lying unconscious on the kitchen floor and knelt quickly to feel her pulse. It was very weak, but she was still alive.

She found Cassie slumped over the dining room table. Her hands were badly cut, as if she had fought off an attacker. Elizabeth gently raised Cassie's head and saw that she had suffered some wounds to her chest, but she too had a pulse.

Mooch the cat finally emerged from underneath an upended chair, crying piteously.

The ambulance was pulling up in front of the house and Elizabeth rushed to the door to let the paramedics in. "There are three of them," she blurted out, half-hysterical. "My mother's awake, but she may have a head injury. Mrs. Wright—she's in her eighties—

is unconscious and her pulse is very weak. She's in the kitchen. Cassie's in the dining room. She's been badly cut. Oh God, please help them."

The paramedics performed triage and carried Mabel by stretcher to the waiting ambulance. She appeared to have suffered a massive coronary, and they sent the ambulance ahead so she could go directly to the hospital's intensive care unit.

Cassie was conscious now, but in shock, and the paramedics moved her next to a second ambulance that the driver had sent for. Then they placed Becca on a stretcher to take her to the hospital.

"Please, can I ride with her?" Elizabeth asked.

"Yes. She'll be confused if she's suffered a concussion. It will be good for her to have a family member present to calm her," one of the paramedics replied.

Elizabeth held her mother's hand and tried to smile at her in spite of her tears. "Oh, Mom. I'm so sorry. I'm so glad we didn't lose you."

"But how did you know to come, Elizabeth?"

"Leah called me. Charlotte had a horrible nightmare and was hysterical. She said the bad men were coming to kill Grandma. Leah kept calling you, but didn't get an answer. She was starting to worry and so she called me and asked if I'd go check on you."

"Dear, sweet Charlotte. I think, for better or worse, she may have inherited my ability to see things."

"But, I don't understand, Mom. Who on earth would attack you?"

"It's a very long story, Elizabeth. I'm just glad you found us in time. Is Mooch okay?"

"He's fine, Mom. Just frightened. I'll go back to check on him later."

The ambulance was now pulling up to the emergency doors of the hospital.

Becca smiled as she looked up at Elizabeth, moving a hand to wipe the tears from her daughter's face. "You'd have been very proud of me, Elizabeth. I was terrified, but I fought them anyway with all my strength."

51

Saturday Afternoon

Elizabeth was sitting beside her mother's hospital bed, quietly reading to her from an old Ray Bradbury novel that she knew her mom loved. They were awaiting the results of the CAT scan to determine the extent of Becca's injuries.

Elizabeth had called Jim and Leah to tell them what had happened. Jim was on his way from Ottawa, but she had convinced Leah that their mom was okay and that she and Charlotte could wait another two weeks until the March break. Leah had agreed reluctantly.

"How are Cassie and Mabel doing, Elizabeth?"

"Cassie was very lucky. The shards of glass didn't penetrate her heart, and her wounds were superficial. They're keeping her overnight anyway because she was in shock when they brought her in. Unfortunately Mabel isn't doing as well. She's still in intensive care and hasn't regained consciousness."

"Can you do me a favour, Elizabeth?" Becca explained what she wanted.

Elizabeth looked skeptical, but said she would try to locate Mabel's doctor. She found him writing up a chart at the nurses' station in the intensive care unit. She repeated her mother's request to him.

"Well, under the circumstances I don't think it could do any harm. I'll talk to the hospital and see if they'll bend the rules a bit."

******

Jane Wright led Tex into the intensive care unit and watched her oldest sister lying motionless on the bed. There was a large glass partition that separated visitors from the patients. Tex stood on his hind legs and placed his paws on the glass. As soon as he saw Mabel, he began to whimper.

"It's okay, boy. I'm sure she knows you're here."

52

The Following Monday

Elizabeth had arranged for the windows and front door lock to be replaced in her mother's house and for a cleaning service to remove the glass debris, clean the carpet, and straighten up the furniture. She sat now with Cassie in the living room.

Becca was out of the hospital, but was resting. She was still prone to headaches and dizziness from the concussion.

Elizabeth had been examining the notebook written by Cassie's mother, as well as the other documents the women had assembled.

Cassie explained, "It all started when King James VI sailed to Copenhagen to marry Anne, the sister of the King of Denmark. On the return voyage, they experienced terrible storms, which were blamed on witchcraft. Witch trials were held in Denmark with many accused of sorcery, and King James decided to convene his own trials in Scotland. The trials were held in North Berwick in 1590."

Elizabeth interjected, "So this street bears the same name as the town in Scotland where all those people died."

"Yes," Cassie said, "and we believe this street was deliberately chosen and all of us brought here for final retribution."

Cassie resumed her account of the trials. "The North Berwick witch trials began with a young maid named Gillis Duncan, who had developed an ability for healing. It was common in all witch trials to condemn such people as being in league with the devil. She was tortured by her employer, David Seaton, into a false confession that she was a witch and into naming others. My mother's maiden name was Seaton, making her one of their prime targets, and I assume that others on this street are descendants of either the townspeople who turned in their neighbours or who sat in judgment in court proceedings.

"The victims were ordinary people suddenly confronted with accusations of witchcraft, and their confessions were extracted through torture authorized by

James VI. One of the first to be accused was Agnes Sampson, a woman who'd been a respected member of the community. She apparently held out as long as she could before being forced to proclaim that she was a witch.

"A school master, John Fian, also confessed to sorcery under extreme torture. And there were many other victims, more than one hundred in total, who were tortured into stating that they were in league with the devil and were guilty of plotting against James VI by attempting to sink his ship."

Elizabeth asked simply, "Is it over?"

Cassie shook her head. "I don't honestly know. But I do know one thing for sure, Elizabeth. Your mother's a very brave woman. If she hadn't intervened, well—

"I'm not certain whether your mother killed the man who was attacking me because the body must have been removed by his companions. But I do know that she saved my life."

53

Wednesday Afternoon/Evening

Mabel Wright had regained consciousness and was now out of intensive care. Her first of many visitors were Becca and Elizabeth Anderson and Cassie Patterson. Each in turn gave her a kiss on the forehead, so glad to see that she was feeling better.

Becca asked, "How are you, Mabel? You gave us all a real scare."

Mabel took Becca's hand. "I think I'll survive. Right, Tex?" She patted the dog's head fondly. "Tex managed to convince me that it wasn't my time yet."

Cassie laughed. "Mrs. Wright, you're a real gem. We could all learn a lot from you."

Looking slightly embarrassed, Mabel said, "Thank you, dear." She leaned over to

Becca and whispered, "Is it finished?"

Becca gave her a tentative smile. "Well, I'm not sure, but my lightning rod isn't registering anything right now. Let's pray it's over."

******

Later that evening, Mabel had a surprise visit from Edna and Nick Harris.

"Well, young man, I finally get a chance to thank you in person for saving me the first time. I seem to have more lives than a cat."

"That's okay, Mrs. Wright. I'm just glad you're feeling better. Hey, what a neat dog. Can I pat him?"

Edna Harris started to object, but Mabel said, "You certainly can, Nick. Tex is an excellent judge of character. I'm sure he'll like you. Edna, would you mind checking at the nurses' station to see if they have any idea when Tex and I can go home? The baby food they're feeding me will be the death of me yet."

As Edna left the room, Mabel turned to Nick. "So, young man, Becca told me you knew when our enemies were coming and warned her. You're a very brave boy indeed. Don't be afraid of your gift, Nick. It makes you very special."

Nick was sitting on the floor, patting Tex, who seemed quite pleased by all of the attention. "Thanks, Mrs. Wright. And it's quiet right now, no more warnings."

"I'm glad to hear that, Nick. And here's hoping that we won't ever have to deal with that lot again."

54

Friday Afternoon

Mabel Wright was finally back at home under the care of a private nurse. She'd asked to see Becca and Cassie. The three women were now sitting in her living room.

"You're looking so much better, Mabel. I can't believe the difference," Becca said.

"It's good to be back home at last. This is where I belong." Mabel patted Tex on the head as she spoke. "But the three of us ladies made a great team, don't you think?"

"We did indeed," Becca replied. "Somehow after all we've been through, it's going to be hard to go back to a 'normal' life. Baking cookies seems a bit anti-climactic to me after all this."

"You used to work for the government before you retired, didn't you?" Cassie asked.

Becca smiled. "Yes, I worked in community services with youth at risk. I've been giving it a great deal of thought lately, wondering if I might be able to go back on a part-time basis. I'd like a chance to work with young people again. See if I can help them. What about you, Cassie?"

"Finding my mother's journal has changed me somehow. I think she was telling me not to feel alone ... to get on with my life. I realize now that I never really let go of her. I've been in mourning all these years. Maybe that's why she's never appeared to me in spirit form. Why she sent the protectors instead."

"Speaking of which, did you learn anything else about your three protectors?" Becca asked.

"Yes, I did. Dietrich had tried to protect my mother, but the adversaries poisoned her before he could intervene. That's why he took a special interest in protecting me. And I think Edward and Jana may have been two of his descendants.

"My mother's journal told me the story of Dietrich. He was another victim of the witch trials, but in Trier, Germany, about the same time as the North Berwick trials. He was Dietrich Flade, Chief Judge of the court that tried the so-called witches. He was against their persecution and torture, and in the end he was tortured and executed himself for his opposition to the trials. But unlike our adversaries, he forgave his tormentors."

"It's tragic that so many people were led astray by misguided religious beliefs into taking part in the witch hunts," Becca said.

Cassie replied, "That was part of it. In the case of the North Berwick witch trials, it was the Protestants under James VI, and later in Salem it was the Puritans. And the Trier witch trials were part of a larger scheme to eliminate all non-conformists to Catholicism.

"But in all of the trials there were economic and political agendas as well. The property of the accused witches was confiscated, and many of the accusers grew rich as a result. From a political perspective, King James VI was trying to establish Protestantism as the only religion in Scotland, and the elimination of Roman Catholics helped quell his opposition."

Cassie shook her head sadly. "And four centuries later, we're still torturing and eliciting false confessions in the name of freedom and democracy, assured that we're on the 'right' side. I don't know when it will ever end."

Becca asked gently, "Where do you go from here, Cassie, knowing all this?"

"My mother said I had a power that could be developed. I was able to use it to quell the fires they set when they attacked us. I'd like to learn if I can use it to do some good in this world."

The three women were silent for a time. Then Cassie asked, "What about you, Mrs. Wright? How do you feel about all that's happened?"

"Well, I have my own soul-searching to do. I have to come to terms with the fact that they were responsible for the deaths of my sons and my husband." Then she added, "I think I'll be okay though. I'm tired and I'm getting on in years, but I'm a tough old bird."

And the other two women smiled knowingly.

55

One Week Later

Roland Fian knelt before the unmarked grave of James Sampson. At Sampson's request, there had been no ceremony, no mourners. At least Angus, Donald, and Scott had been buried by their families.

In the end Roland had opted to tell his old friend a lie so he could die in peace, if such a state were possible for James Sampson.

In truth, the women had not been mortally wounded, and he'd heard that even the old one had recovered.

The remaining Guardians of Truth had fled. They'd had no appetite for further violence. They wanted to lead normal lives again. And who could really blame them? Many of them had families and had never been strongly committed to the cause, anyway.

And what about me? Do I honour my friend's death by continuing the battle? Surely there are others I can recruit to rebuild our circle. Or am I as sick of violence as the ones who fled?

He placed a small bouquet of wildflowers on the burial mound and then stood up, lingering for a few moments in front of his friend's grave.

Then he turned and, lost in thought, walked quietly away.

Acknowledgments

I would like to thank my husband Mike McCann for his support at every stage of this book. He not only read the draft and offered suggestions for its improvement, but also designed the covers and performed the necessary work for its publication. He did all of this in between his own writing. Once again, Mike, thanks for everything.

In addition, I'd like to thank my readers, Margaret Leroux, Melanie Robertson-King, and Katherine Hooton for their excellent feedback.

I would also like to extend a special thanks to Heather Jones, to whom this book is dedicated, for her ongoing support for my husband's writing and mine.

When I started doing the research for this novel, I had planned to base the story on the Salem witch trials, which have always fascinated me. In addition to my online research, I'd read two well-regarded books on the trials, *In the Devil's Snare* (Vintage reprint, 2003) by Mary Beth Norton and *A Delusion of Satan: The Full Story of the Salem Witch Trials* (Doubleday, 1995) by Frances Hill. Norton's book postulates that the witchcraft trials must be examined in the broader context of King

William's War (known as the Second Indian War by early Americans) and the effects it had on those involved in the Salem trials. Hill's book examines various factors that may have contributed to the witch trials, including the repressive theology of the Puritan religion, the constant fear of attack during the Second Indian War, and the economic and political struggles between the families of the accusers and those of the accused.

A recent account of the Salem trials is *The Witches: Salem, 1692* (Little, Brown and Company, 2015) by Stacy Schiff, which contains detailed information on source documents, as well as an extensive bibliography of works relating to the witch trials.

As my research progressed, I decided that I wanted to base my story on the European witch trials, which have received much less attention in fiction, but which predated the Salem trials and claimed thousands of victims. Being of Scottish heritage, I chose the North Berwick trials as my starting point.

For information on the transformation of witchcraft as a tolerated form of folk magic to its identification with Satanism and heresy in the early modern period, please refer to https://en.wikipedia. org/wiki/Witch_trials_in_ the_early_modern_ period. The peak of the trials occurred between 1580 and 1630. The majority of those accused were from the lower economic class, although some priests, judges, and members of the nobility were also accused of sorcery. Witch trials in Ireland and England were less frequent, while in Scotland James VI took a particular interest in the trials, authorizing the use of torture to extract confessions. An estimated 75 to 85 per cent of those persecuted in the early witch trials were women, although in some trials, it was primarily men who were accused of witchcraft. In all, it is estimated that between 40,000 and 60,000 people were executed in the witch trials.

For information on the term "moral panic," see https://en.wikipedia.org/wiki/Moral_panic. As noted in this article, the use of the word "moral" to describe such occurrences has been criticized.

For the North Berwick witch trials, see https://en.wikipedia.org/wiki/North_Berwick_ witch_ trials. Please see also *Newes from Scotland*, a contemporary account of the North Berwick witch trials published as a pamphlet in 1591 and reprinted at http://www.sacred-texts.com/pag/kjd/kjd11.htm. The author is believed to be James Carmichael, who helped interrogate the witches in the North Berwick trials and also advised King James VI on the writing of his book on witchcraft, *Daemonologie*.

Information and links to scholarly websites on the history of witchcraft and witch-hunting in Scotland may be found at the University of Edinburgh website: http://www.shca.ed.ac.uk/

Research/witches/illustration.html and http://www.shca.ed.ac.uk/Research/ witches/links.html.

The information on witchcraft in the Scottish Archive Network at http://www.scan.org.uk/exhibitions/witchhunt_contents.htm is particularly interesting with its images and transcripts of burgh records relating to later Scottish witch trials.

Details from these various reference sources have been adapted for this novel, and you will recognize some of the surnames of the accused among the Guardians of Truth, including Sampson, Fian, Napier, Grierson, Motts, and Thompson. The Guardians of Truth is a fictitious group created for the sake of the story. There is no intended relationship with any existing organizations that have adopted the same name.

The Scottish genealogy site referenced in this novel as containing records dating back to 1513 is found at http://www.scotlandspeople.gov.uk/.

The protector Dietrich, as noted in the novel, is based on Dietrich Flade, who tried to use his position of authority to help those accused of witchcraft in the Trier witch trials in Germany, but who became one of the persecuted. For information on the Trier witch trials, please see https://en.wikipedia.org/wiki/Trier_witch_trials. This was one of the largest witch trials in Europe with almost 400 executions in this city alone. Many more were executed in the surrounding diocese.

For information on the Wiccan faith and

the symbolism of the pentagram, please refer to https://en.wikipedia.org/wiki/Wicca. As noted in this article, Wicca represents a wide range of beliefs. For the Wiccan Rede (meaning advice or counsel), which is accepted by some but not all Wiccans, see https://en.wikipedia.org/wiki/ Wiccan_Rede.

For the significance of the number three, I have referred to http://www.betemunah. org/ three.html and to http://numerology-thenumbersandtheirmeanings.blogspot.ca/2011/ 02/number-3.html.

The Wiccan Rule of Three is discussed at https://en.wikipedia.org/wiki/Rule_of_ Three_%28Wicca%29.

For white magic circles, spells, and protection against black magic, I have consulted numerous sites, including https://en.wikipedia.org/wiki/ White_magic; http://www.nairaland.com/ 301568/magic-spells-understanding-how-use; http://www.spellsandmagic.com/; and http:// www.thesmartwitch.com/The_Smart_Witch_ Magic_Spell.html. I found the "Smart Witch" site particularly helpful because it includes information on the use of white, black, and green candles to cleanse the body of negative energy, as well as on the ancient belief in the importance of knowing an adversary's true name to exert power over him. It also has information on what herbs are used in magic.

I consulted the following sources for information on the Ouija board: http://www.paranormality. com/ouija_board.shtml and https://en.wikipedia. org/wiki/Ouija.

For information on the Sigil of Baphomet used by the Church of Satan, please see https:// en.wikipedia.org/wiki/Sigil_of_Baphomet.

For information on physical and sexual abuse at the St. Joseph's Training School for Boys in Alfred, Ontario, run by the Christian Brothers' Schools of Ottawa, please refer to http://www. religioustolerance.org/clergy_sex3b.htm; http:// poundpuplegacy.org/; and http://www.cbc.ca/ news/canada/victims-of-abuse-at-ontario-school-get-1-million-settlement-1.490479. When the abuse first came to light, I read in the local paper that one of the many victims had committed suicide in Stony Mountain Prison, Manitoba. The account of Jim Anderson's client is based loosely on this man's death, in recognition of the abuse he suffered.

When writing this novel, I also had in mind Ray Bradbury's *Something Wicked This Way Comes*. I read this book when I was in my early thirties, and the pathos of Charles Halloway, a man in his fifties with a young son who yearns for his lost youth, has resonated with me throughout the years. Who among us, faced with the realities of aging, would not be tempted to ride the carousel backward? I would like to think that there is something of Charles Halloway in Rebecca Anderson, an average person recognizing that she is growing old and questioning what she has done with her life, but still trying to do the right thing by fighting an evil that threatens her family and friends. The lightning rod symbol in *Something Wicked This Way Comes* has been adapted by me for this novel. The term "soul's midnight" for 3 AM is used in the Bradbury novel, and it is from this book that Elizabeth reads to her mother in the hospital. The power of laughter as a weapon against evil is also a central theme in Bradbury's novel, as well as being discussed on the white magic sites I consulted.

The dream experienced by Mabel in this novel is based on one of my own that I had while writing this book. The only change I've made is to have the angel children appear with the faces of Mabel's dead twins.

Last but not least, Mabel's dog Tex is based on my own dog Tex, who died long ago, but who is never far from my thoughts.

About the Author

Lynn Clark was born in Woodstock, New Brunswick, Canada. She received her B.A. and M.A. from Acadia University in Wolfville, Nova Scotia. Prior to her retirement in 2011, she worked for almost thirty years for the federal government in Ottawa, Ontario, Canada. She lives in a small town in eastern Ontario with her husband, crime fiction writer Michael J. McCann. She is also the author of *The Home Child* and *Fire Whisperer and Circle of Souls: Two Novellas of the Supernatural.*

If you enjoyed
The Accusers
by Lynn L. Clark

You will also want to read her exciting first novel

The
Home Child
a supernatural novel

*what if you
could never go
home again?*

Lynn L. Clark

If you enjoyed
The Accusers
by Lynn L. Clark

You will also want to read her exciting double feature